THIS WALKER BOOK BELONGS TO:

_____

_____

_____

For sweet dreams…

First published 2003 by Walker Books Ltd
87 Vauxhall Walk, London SE11 5HJ

This edition published 2004

6 8 10 9 7

This book has been typeset in Berling

Printed in China

British Library Cataloguing in Publication Data:
a catalogue record for this book is available from the British Library

ISBN 978-1-8442-8500-6

www.walkerbooks.co.uk

Goodnight, Harry

Kim Lewis

WALKER BOOKS
AND SUBSIDIARIES
LONDON · BOSTON · SYDNEY · AUCKLAND

Harry the elephant
was getting ready for bed
with his friends,
Lulu and Ted.

"Goodnight, everyone," said Harry.

"Zzz," went Lulu.

"Snore," went Ted.

Harry lay waiting.

But sleep didn't come.

"I forgot my bedtime story,"

thought Harry.

He opened his books.
He looked at the pictures.

He looked at the words.
His eyes grew heavy.

He snuggled down again.
"I'm waiting," he said.
But sleep didn't
come to Harry.

"Perhaps I'm not really tired,"
thought Harry.

He hung up his clothes.　　He tidied his room.

He ran on the spot.

He touched his toes.

He hopped on one foot.

He jumped up and down.

Then Harry got back into bed.

"Zzz," went Lulu.

"Snore," went Ted.

"I'm waiting," said Harry.

But nothing happened.

"Perhaps I'm not really comfy," thought Harry.

He stretched out
one way.

He stretched out
the other.

He lay on his tummy.
He lay on his back.

He closed his eyes tight.

"Zzz," went Lulu.

"Snore," went Ted.

"I'm still awake," sighed Harry.

Then Harry began to worry.

He worried and worried.

He just couldn't stop.

He thought of tomorrow.

He thought of today.

He thought about nothing.

He thought about lots.

He wriggled and squiggled.

He rolled in a ball …

and he took all the blankets.

"Hey!" said Lulu,
waking up with a start.
"Harry, what are you doing?" said Ted.

"I can't get to sleep,"
said Harry sadly.

Harry looked out of the window.

He rubbed his tired eyes.

"What if sleep never ever
comes at all?" he said.

"Never mind, Harry," said Lulu.
"We're here, Harry," said Ted.

The three little friends sat close together.

They looked at the world outside.

Lulu sang a song to the moon.

Ted counted the bright evening stars.

They heard an owl hoot.

Petals fell in the breeze.

They felt the dew of the night.

Harry snuggled up with
Lulu and Ted.

His eyes felt heavy.
He gave a big yawn.

"Goodnight, Harry," said Lulu.

"Sweet dreams, Harry," said Ted.

But Harry was fast asleep,
and "Snuffle" was all he said.

WALKER BOOKS is the world's leading
independent publisher of children's books.
Working with the best authors and illustrators
we create books for all ages, from babies
to teenagers – books your child will
grow up with and always remember. So…

FOR THE BEST CHILDREN'S BOOKS,
LOOK FOR THE BEAR